# Daisy's Bell

BY MICHÈLE DUFRESNE

Pioneer Valley Educational Press, Inc.

One day, Bella, Rosie,
Jack, and Daisy
went outside to play.

*Ring, ring! Ring, ring!*

"What was that?" asked Bella.
"Listen, Rosie."

Rosie stopped and listened.

*Ring, ring! Ring, ring!*

Bella looked at Daisy.
"Is Daisy ringing?" she asked Rosie.

Rosie looked at Daisy's collar.
"She has a bell on her collar,"
said Rosie.

"A bell? How silly!" said Bella.

"Go away and play with Jack,"
Bella said to Daisy.

"Let's take a nap," said Bella.

"Good idea," said Rosie.

"Rosie, wake up! Bella, wake up!
I can't find Daisy. She's missing!"
cried Jack.

Rosie and Bella woke up.
They both looked around.
They did not see Daisy anywhere.

"Daisy, where are you?" called Rosie.

"Oh, dear! Oh, dear!
Maybe she is lost,"
cried Rosie.
"Come on, we need to find her."

Bella and Rosie ran across the yard
to look for Daisy.

"Daisy! Daisy!" called Rosie.
"Where are you, Daisy?"

*Ring, ring! Ring, ring!*

"What was that?" said Rosie.
"Listen, Bella!"

Bella stopped and listened.

*Ring, ring! Ring, ring!*

"I hear that silly bell," said Bella.

"Me, too," said Rosie.
"Come on, now we can find her."

*Ring, ring! Ring, ring!*

"Look! Here she is," said Rosie.

"Hmm, Daisy's bell is silly,
but it helped us find her!" said Bella.